This book belongs to:

....

....

A NEW BURLINGTON BOOK
The Old Brewery
6 Blundell Street
London N7 9BH

Editor: Alexandra Koken
Designer: Plum Pudding Design

Copyright © QEB Publishing 2012

First published in the United States by
QEB Publishing
3 Wrigley, Suite A
Irvine, CA 92618

www.qed-publishing.co.uk

A CIP record for this book is available from the Library of Congress.

ISBN 978 1 78171 264 1

Printed in China

My Friend the
Weather Monster

Steve Smallman and Bruno Merz

NEW
BURLINGTON
BOOKS

In a dark, dreary cave,
high up on a mountain, lived...
the Weather Monster.

When he felt happy, the sun shone.
When he felt sad, it rained.
And it had rained a lot lately.

"How can we cheer up the Weather Monster and get some sunshine?" asked the soggy villagers down in the valley.

"Let's make him a cake!" cried Tom, the baker's boy.
"Great idea!" everyone agreed.
But they were all too frightened to deliver it.

Early the next morning, shaking with fear,
Tom climbed up the mountain. He carried
a huge cake in his backpack.

Tom reached the monster's cave. He was about
to ring the bell when a soft voice surprised him.

"Hello," said the Weather Monster.
"My name's Ron. What's yours?"
"Eek!" yelped Tom.

"Nice to meet you, Eek," said the Weather Monster.
"Would you like some tea?"

"Er, okay," said Tom.
"And I've brought you a cake from the village!"

The Weather Monster smiled
and the sun came out.

"Why hasn't anybody come to visit me before?"
asked the Weather Monster.
"Well, they think you're a little...scary," said Tom.

"Oh," sniffed the Weather Monster.
"So why did they send me a cake?"
"Because they wanted to cheer you up..."
said Tom, "...and get some sunshine."

"SUNSHINE?"

shouted the Weather Monster angrily.

"THEY DON'T CARE ABOUT HOW I FEEL. THEY JUST WANT THE RIGHT WEATHER!"

Thunder roared
and lightning flashed.
Tom was scared.

"Oh, I'm sorry!" sniffed the Weather Monster.
"I didn't mean to frighten you.
I just get so lonely up here, and I hoped that
maybe they wanted to be my friends."

"But I'm sure they do!" cried Tom.
"Come down to the village with me and you'll see!"

When the villagers saw the Weather Monster
lumbering toward them, they were scared.

But then they saw Tom, sitting on the monster's
shoulders with a big smile on his face.
"Meet my friend Ron!" Tom called.

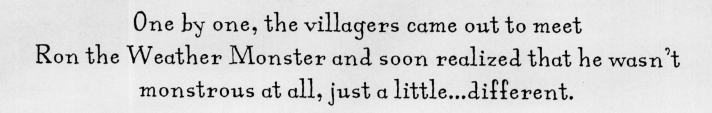

One by one, the villagers came out to meet
Ron the Weather Monster and soon realized that he wasn't
monstrous at all, just a little...different.

"Live here with us!"
cried Tom, and everyone agreed.
"Thank you," smiled Ron.
"But I think I might be a bit big to live here."

So, from then on, the villagers
took turns visiting Ron's cave for
tea and cake almost every day.

But nobody called him the Weather
Monster anymore. He was Ron, their friend.

And the sun shone.

Next Steps

Show the children the cover again. Did the children think the story would be scary because it's about a monster?

How do the children feel about the Weather Monster now that they have read the story?

Ask the children what words they would use to describe the Weather Monster.

Ask the children to each draw a monster.

Why are the villagers in the story so scared of the Weather Monster? Are they less scared of him when they find out his name?

Ask the children what kinds of things make them scared. Discuss what it feels like to be lonely or left out.

If the children could control the weather, what type of weather would they choose?